DINOSAUR WORLD

PTERANODON

Aaron Carr and
John Willis

AV2
www.av2books.com

Step 1
Go to **www.av2books.com**

Step 2
Enter this unique code
SFOCR51XZ

Step 3
Explore your interactive eBook!

AV2 is optimized for use on any device

Your interactive eBook comes with...

Contents
Browse a live contents page to easily navigate through resources

Audio
Listen to sections of the book read aloud

Videos
Watch informative video clips

Weblinks
Gain additional information for research

Try This!
Complete activities and hands-on experiments

Key Words
Study vocabulary, and complete a matching word activity

Quizzes
Test your knowledge

Slideshows
View images and captions

This title is part of our AV2 digital subscription

1-Year Grades K–5 Subscription
ISBN 978-1-7911-3320-7

Access hundreds of AV2 titles with our digital subscription.
Sign up for a FREE trial at **www.av2books.com/trial**

PTERANODON

CONTENTS

Winged and Toothless

Pteranodon is one of the best known of all **prehistoric** flying reptiles. Its name means "winged and toothless." *Pteranodon* had a sleek, featherless body and a **crest** on the back of its head.

Scientists are not sure if *Pteranodon* was scaled, like modern-day reptiles, or if it was covered in fur. *Pteranodon* is often incorrectly called a pterodactyl. However, this name fits a much smaller flying reptile, *Pterodactylus*, instead.

Pterosaurs

***P**teranodon* was not a dinosaur. It was part of a group of reptiles called pterosaurs. Unlike dinosaurs, pterosaurs could fly. Pterosaurs had **hollow** bones, relatively large brains, and good eyesight. Their hollow bones helped keep their bodies light in weight.

Pterosaurs were found in what are now the continents of North America, Africa, Europe, and Australia. They ranged in size from just a few inches (centimeters) to the giant *Quetzalcoatlus*, which was as tall as a giraffe and had an airplane-sized wingspan.

Large Wingspan

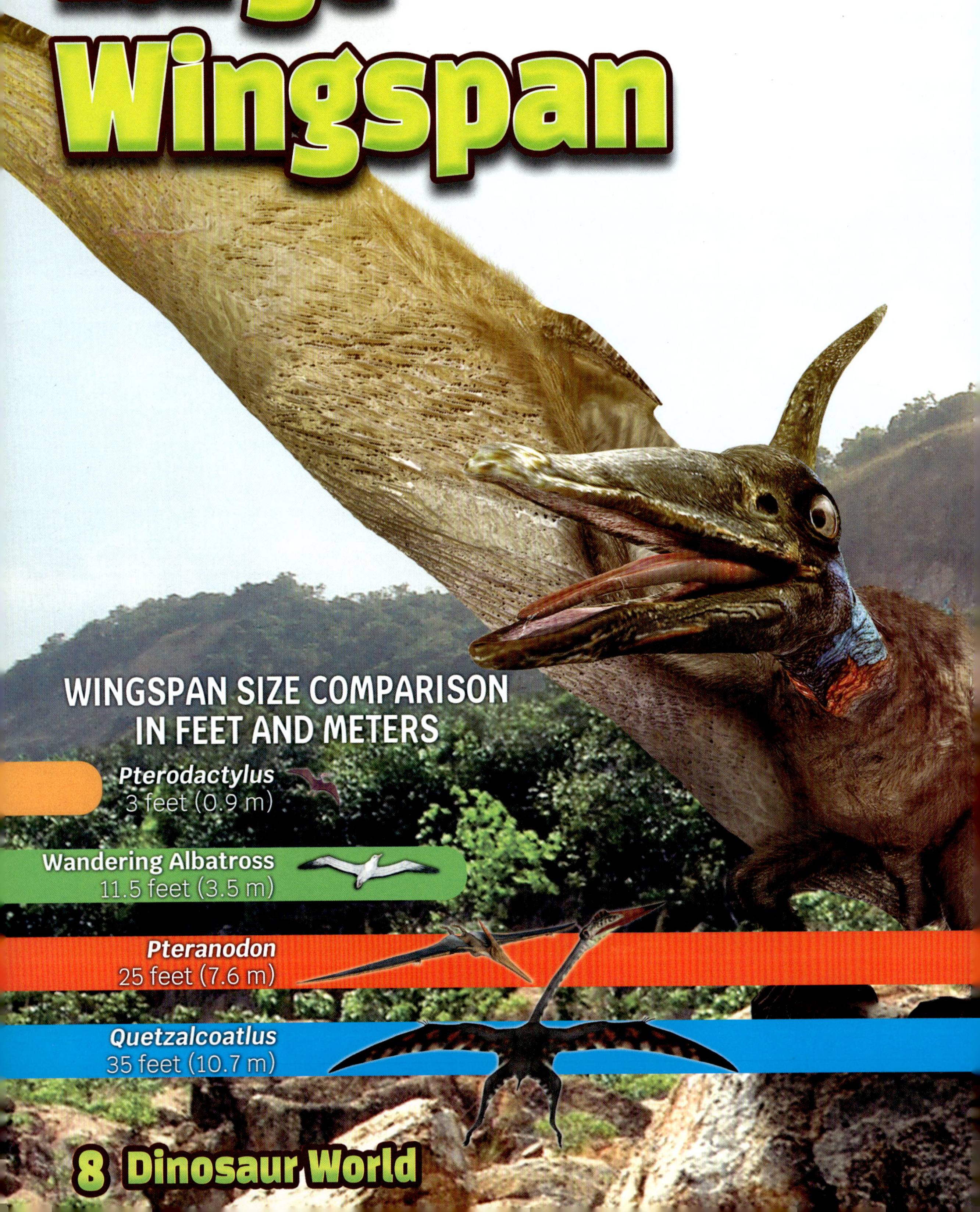

WINGSPAN SIZE COMPARISON IN FEET AND METERS

Pterodactylus
3 feet (0.9 m)

Wandering Albatross
11.5 feet (3.5 m)

Pteranodon
25 feet (7.6 m)

Quetzalcoatlus
35 feet (10.7 m)

Pteranodon was considered a medium-sized pterosaur. However, it was still larger than any flying bird today. It could have a wingspan more than twice the size of that of a modern-day albatross.

Pteranodon's wings were made up of leathery **membranes** stretched over its arms and hands. An extremely long fourth finger made up a large part of each wing.

Meat Eater

Pteranodon was a **carnivore**. It mostly fed on fish and other animals that lived in water. *Pteranodon* did not just eat **aquatic** animals, though. It sometimes ate insects, especially during its first few years of life. Scientists believe *Pteranodon* even **scavenged** for dead animals it found lying on the ground.

Toothless Jaw

Pteranodon had a very long jaw with no teeth. It is believed that *Pteranodon* hunted for fish the same way pelicans do today. *Pteranodon* would have flown above the water and used its beak to snatch up fish swimming just below the surface. Without teeth, *Pteranodon* was not able to chew its food. Instead, it had to swallow its meals whole.

Soaring Flight

By studying *Pteranodon*'s wings and bones, scientists have determined that it relied more on **soaring** than flapping during flight. The crest on *Pteranodon*'s head may have acted as a **rudder** to help it steer in the air.

Pteranodon's **streamlined** body was fairly small compared to the size of its wings. This meant that on the ground, *Pteranodon* was not much taller than a person. A small body helped *Pteranodon* glide for long distances, much like the largest modern-day flying birds.

HEIGHT COMPARISON
Pteranodon
6 feet
(1.8 m)
Human
5.6 feet
(1.7 m)

Habitat

Pteranodon lived near large bodies of water in North America and Europe. Due to its primarily aquatic diet, *Pteranodon* preferred to stay close to the shores of oceans, rivers, or lakes.

Scientists have found evidence that *Pteranodon* may have gathered in large numbers inside caves. They have also suggested that it used the claws on its winged hands to anchor itself to cliff faces.

Fossilization

Pteranodon lived about 100 million years ago. This time was known as the Late Cretaceous Period. *Pteranodon* died out so long ago that people only know about it from its bones, which turned into **fossils** over millions of years.

Steps of Fossilization

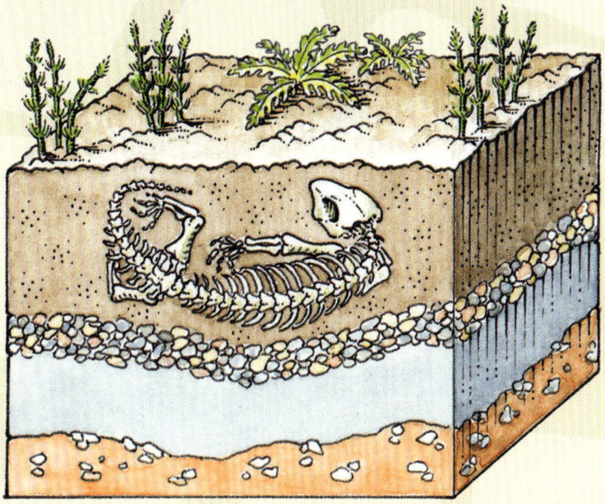

1 An animal dies and is quickly covered in sand, mud, or water. This keeps the hard parts of the body, such as bones, teeth, and claws, from **decomposing**.

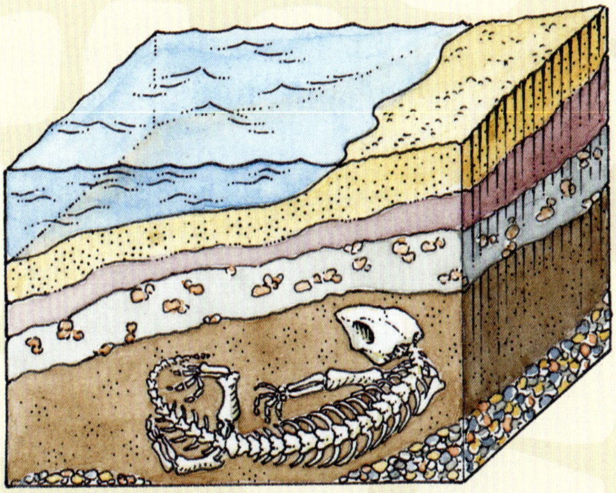

2 The body is pressed between layers of mud and sand.

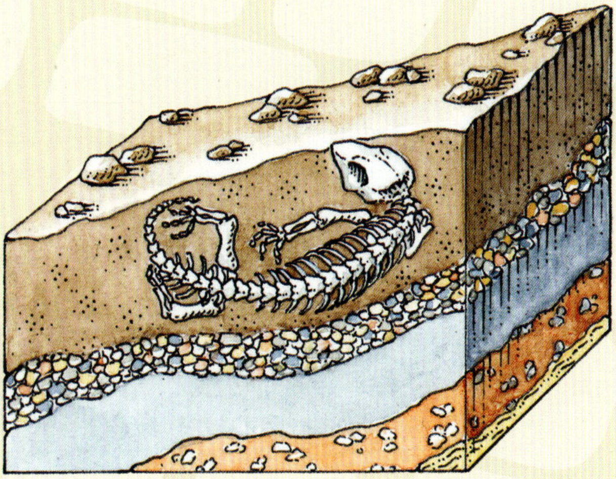

3 Over millions of years, the layers turn into stone. The animal's bones and teeth turn into stone as well. This **preserves** the animal's size and shape.

At the Museum

See For Yourself

Visitors to Kansas's Sternberg Museum of Natural History can see the third-largest collection of pterosaur fossils on Earth.

People can go to museums to see fossils and learn more about *Pteranodon*. Millions of people around the world visit museums each year to see dinosaur and pterosaur fossils in person.

Pteranodon displays can be found in large museums worldwide, including the National Museum of Natural History in Washington, D.C., and even in much smaller museums, such as the Sternberg Museum of Natural History in Kansas.

Quiz

1
What did *Pteranodon* mostly eat?

2
Do scientists think *Pteranodon* was covered in fur or with scales?

3
How many teeth did *Pteranodon* have?

4
How long ago did *Pteranodon* live?

5
How large was *Pteranodon*'s wingspan?

6
What does *Pteranodon* mean?

7
On which modern continents did *Pteranodon* live?

8
How might *Pteranodon*'s crest have helped it fly?

ANSWERS
1. Fish 2. They are not sure. 3. None 4. About 100 million years ago 5. 25 feet (7.6 m) 6. "Winged and toothless" 7. North America and Europe 8. By acting as a rudder

Key Words

aquatic: growing or living in water

carnivore: an animal that only eats meat

crest: a ridge or tuft on an animal's body

decomposing: breaking down or rotting

fossils: remains from living things that have turned to stone over many years

hollow: having an unfilled, empty space within

membranes: thin sheets or layers of tissue

prehistoric: before known history

preserves: stops something from decomposing

rudder: part of a boat or airplane that turns to make the vehicle turn

scavenged: fed on something that had already died

soaring: flying by using upward-moving air currents

streamlined: shaped to move through air or water easily

Index

Published by AV2
276 5th Avenue, Suite 704 #917
New York, NY 10001
Website: www.av2books.com

Library of Congress Control Number: 2020951633

ISBN 978-1-7911-3443-3 (hardcover)
ISBN 978-1-7911-3444-0 (softcover)
ISBN 978-1-7911-3445-7 (multi-user eBook)

Printed in Guangzhou, China
1 2 3 4 5 6 7 8 9 0 25 24 23 22 21

022021
101120

Designer: Terry Paulhus **Project Coordinator:** John Willis

Every reasonable effort has been made to trace ownership and to obtain permission to reprint copyright material. The publisher would be pleased to have any errors or omissions brought to its attention so that they may be corrected in subsequent printings.

AV2 acknowledges Getty Images and Jon Hughes, pixel-shack.com, as the primary image suppliers for this title.